Stray

by

David Belbin

Illustrated by Julia Page

Published in 2006 in Great Britain by
Barrington Stoke Ltd
18 Walker Street, Edinburgh, EH3 7LP

www.barringtonstoke.co.uk

Reprinted 2007

ISBN: 978-1-84299-381-1

Printed in Great Britain by Bell & Bain Ltd

A Note from the Author

Why did I write this story? I started off thinking about girls in gangs. Then I thought about how some people seem to get away with everything. But there are others who can't put even a foot wrong without getting into trouble.

Life isn't fair. A few things come down to luck. But most things come down to the choices you make.

Stacey and Simone are based on young women I knew once. They were always in trouble. One of them was playing at being a bad girl. For the other, it wasn't a game.

Trouble is, some people have more choices than others. When life treats you like a toilet, it's hard to have morals. And the weaker you are, the more people will try to use you. That's what *Stray* is about.

For Harry Wood

Contents

Prologue

I was about to pay. Behind me, in the corner shop, three girls messed about. They threw stuff around. Crisps. Bottles. Cans of drink.

The shopkeeper called out. “Stop that!”

Simone, the girls' leader, opened the shop door. "Stay!" Simone called. "Stay!"

Was she calling a dog? Then I saw Stacey. She was outside the shop, looking in. Stacey saw me watching. She gave me this shy smile and it hit me like a rocket. Simone threw her a four-pack. Stacey snatched it. Simone rushed out. She was followed by tall Karla and ugly Tracy. Both had a four-pack of lager in each hand. Those two had been in Simone's gang since the start of Year Seven. But not Stacey.

The four of them raced off down the street, giggling like little kids.

The shopkeeper ran into the street. He looked mad. I went after him. “You know those girls?” he asked.

“No. Sorry, mate,” I said.

“Will you talk to the police? Be a witness?”

“Sorry,” I said.

Chapter 1
A Girl I Used to Know

It was five years since I'd seen Stacey. She was in the year below me at primary school. Kids said she was fostered, like me. That's one reason I remembered her. Like me, she was always on her own. Unlike me, she didn't seem to mind.

Most of all, I remembered how very pretty Stacey was. Back then, I never spoke to her. She was too young and she was a girl. Back then, I liked her. Now, I could not get her out of my mind. She had a great body, long blonde hair and an amazing smile. I had to see her again.

But I didn't know where to find her. There were four schools she might go to. I couldn't hang around outside all of them, hoping to spot her. So I had to talk to Simone.

I knew where to find Simone. She was down the playing field, every lunch and break, with the smokers.

"That was you in the shop yesterday, wasn't it?" Simone said. "Have you come to blackmail me?"

"I didn't think you'd seen me," I said.

"I didn't. Stay did."

"Why do you call her 'Stay'?" I asked.

"I can't have a Stacey and a Tracy in my crew. It sounds silly. What's it to you, anyway?"

"I wondered what school Stacey goes to?"

Simone teased me. "Little Kev fancies Stay!"

"I just asked what school she went to."

"Were you at primary with her?" Simone asked.

"How did you know that?" I asked.

"Stay told me," Simone said. "Want me to give her a message?"

I wrote my mobile number on the back of an empty fag packet. Then the bell went. I had Science at the other side of school. I had to hurry. But I looked back. Just in time to see Simone throw the packet away.

Chapter 2
Live and Let Live

I wasn't little, like Simone said. I was about five foot six, and so was Stacey. OK, I hadn't had a girlfriend before. That was the same with most lads in Year Eleven. Simone and her gang were younger than us, but they went out with much older boys. Boys who used them for a bit, then passed them on like CDs. Play them a few times until you get bored of them, then get another. I couldn't bear to see Stacey treated that way.

It was only a crush, I told myself. I had exams to worry about. Girls could wait. But I'd never had a crush before. I thought about Stacey all the time. First thing in the morning. Last thing at night. Every lesson. While I was watching TV. Even when I went to the loo. I didn't know a girl could get under my skin that way. I had to see her.

Next day, I went up to Simone and said:

"Did you give her my number?"

"Who? Stay? I told you, Kev. Not a hope in hell."

"There must be something I can do?"

Simone thought for a moment. "Have you got a bike?" she asked.

"Yeah."

“Turn up at the Black Lion, tonight, at six,” Simone said.

I got to the pub at five to six.

“Stay isn’t allowed out,” Simone told me. “But you can take her a message if you like.”

“All right,” I said. She told me the number of a flat on the estate, and how to find it. Then she gave me a small packet.

“Is this for Stacey?” I asked.

"Just deliver it where I told you," Simone said.

I didn't use drugs, but half the estate did. "Live and let live" would have to be my motto. I'd do anything to get close to Stacey. So I cycled to the block of flats.

The address was on the third floor. I carried my bike up there with me, to be safe.

The door opened.

"Is Stacey there?"

A big hand grabbed the packet. The door slammed shut. I left.

"Nice one," Simone said, when I got back to the pub.

"Stacey wasn't there," I protested.

"She might be at this place," Simone said, handing me another packet. "Why don't you go and see?"

"Only if you give me her mobile number," I said.

Simone thought about it. "Sorry," she said. "I promised not to. I'll tell you where she lives – when you get back."

Chapter 3
Kiss Me, Baby

Stacey wasn't in the next flat I visited. It made me angry. I knew Simone was playing me. She played everyone.

It was a hot, late summer evening, not quite dusk. I cycled slowly. I didn't want to talk to Simone again. Then I saw a girl walking. I slowed down. She was on the dark side of the street. She wore a hoody. That was odd, in the heat. I called her name. The girl turned and my heart jumped.

"Kev, isn't it?" Stacey said.

I nodded. "I remember you from primary, Stacey."

"Don't call me Stacey," she said. Her voice was low, shy, like she was ashamed of herself or something. "I hate it."

"What do I call you if I don't call you Stacey?"

"People in the gang call me 'Stay'," she said.

"That's not a name."

Up close, I saw she had a little gold band on one side of her nose. Her eyes were deep blue. When they met mine, there was a spark. I heard a car coming down the street.

NO BALL
GAMES

"Quick!" Stacey said. "Kiss me!"

In my hurry, I nearly fell off the bike. Her chest pressed hard against mine. We had a huge kiss that lasted ages.

I'd never kissed a girl before, not properly. Stacey was an amazing kisser. No, that's wrong. It takes two to make a kiss. The two of us were amazing.

"It's OK," she said when we broke apart. "They've gone."

"Who've gone?"

"The police. I'm on an ASBO. If I'm out on the street after eight, they can put me back in a detention centre."

"Oh, I see," I said. Though I didn't see.

"What did you get done for?" I asked.

"Just mucking about," she said. "I was the last to get away. I didn't snitch. So they came down hard on me."

"That's a pity," I said. "I'd like to see more of you, St ..."

"What are you going to call me?" she said, softly.

That was when I worked it out. "Stray," I said.

"What?"

"*Stray*," I said.

"Why?"

"It sounds like you. You've got a kind of lost look. Even in a gang, you're on your own."

Stacey nodded. "I like that. Yeah, you can call me 'Stray', Kev. Now I have to go see Simone."

"Want a ride on the back of my bike?"

"No. Too easy to spot me. Tell you what, you ride ahead, make sure there's no police around."

"OK," I said. "But take this first." I wrote down my mobile number and gave it to her.

"I'll call you," she said. Then she kissed me on the cheek and gave me this look that promised everything. I mean *everything.*

As soon as we got to the pub, Simone and Stray got into a car with some older lads. I still didn't have Stray's address or phone number. But I'd kissed her. She wanted me. I felt like a king.

Chapter 4

You Can't Always Get What You Want

I knew Stray was too good looking for a guy like me. "Aim for the best," my mum always told me. "There's no shame in failing. The shame is in not trying." And Stray was the best.

"You said you'd give me Stacey's address," I told Simone at morning break.

"It's not Stacey, it's Stray," Simone said. "She told us. You renamed her. Good choice, Kev. Her boyfriend likes it."

"She hasn't got a boyfriend," I said.

"A girl like Stray can have any lad she wants. Older lads."

"I'm older than her. I'm 16 next week!"

"But you don't have a car," Simone said. "Tell you what. You helped last night. Come round the Lion at seven. I'll sort you out."

Simone was my only way to Stray. So I said I'd go.

Just before I went out, my mobile rang.

"Hi," her shy, sexy voice said. "It's Stray."

"How are you?" I asked.

"OK. Sorry I had to go off like that. But I can't be seen on the street."

"Who were the lads you were with?" I asked.

In the background, I heard a doorbell ring.

"Sorry, babes, gotta go. Catch you later."

She hung up. No caller ID.

****

A gang of girls were sitting on the wall by the pub car park.

"Do you go to school with Stray?" I asked one of them.

"Stray's never at school," the girl said. "What's your name?"

Before I could tell her, a car came by. Simone ran over and talked to the driver. He had a shaved head and a tattoo on his arm. I heard Simone call him "Martin". Then I saw a small figure, hunched up next to him. Stray. The car drove off. Simone came over to me. She handed me two packets and a slip of paper with three addresses on it.

"Deliver these to the first two addresses. There'll be somebody waiting for you at the third address in an hour."

"Stray?"

"You'll get what you deserve," Simone said.

Then a police car came by to move the girls on. I rode off before they saw me.

Everyone does stupid things when they're young. No one thinks they'll get caught. Young and in love? Twice as stupid. I made the drops, then went to the address Simone had given me.

I didn't know the girl who came to the door. She was young. Year Nine maybe. Pretty, too. A bit like Stray, only this girl was a Seven out of Ten and Stray was at least a Nine.

"Are you Kev?" she said.

"Yeah."

"I'm Lucy. Simone said to look after you."

She took my hand and gently pulled me inside. It was an empty flat with a dirty mattress on the floor. Lucy stroked my hair.

"You're nice," she said.

"You're nice too," I said. "But I'm into someone else."

"Simone said I could hang with her if I was nice to you," Lucy said. "Simone's really hooked up. Her and her mates always have a really cool time. Please."

"Can't," I said. "But listen. Whatever Simone tells you to do, don't do it."

I left before I was tempted to change my mind.

Chapter 5
The Things We Do for Love

The next weekend, Stray rang me. Her voice was a bit edgy. It sounded like she had someone with her.

"My ASBO runs out on Monday," she said. "Simone says you're nearly 16. What day's your birthday?"

"Thursday."

"Then you'll be older than me again. I like older boys. Let's party. But before that, could you give us a hand?"

"Anything," I said. I wanted to believe she wanted me.

"Meet me at the shopping centre at two on Wednesday."

"We have games then."

"Skive off. Wear a baseball cap and bring a scarf. OK?"

"I don't understand."

"You don't have to. And come on your bike."

Stray hung up. Again, she'd withheld the number she was calling from. I wanted to tell her the way I felt. But that would have to wait until Wednesday. I'd do whatever she wanted me to do. Stacey wanted to see me on my birthday! She was bound to kiss me again. And more. Maybe much, much more. For the next hour, I played loud music and crashed around my room like a dog on heat.

Chapter 6
Crime of the Century

Simone was there. So were Tracy, Karla and Stray. Stray had her hair down and wore a low cut top. She looked fantastic. All four girls were laughing loudly.

"What's so funny?" I asked.

"The plan," Stray said. "It's like what we did at the corner shop, only bigger. Much, much bigger."

"That's right," Simone said. "And you're our getaway man."

"But I don't drive."

"You can't get a car into the shopping centre," Stray said.

Simone explained the plan. They were going to go to the jeweller's shop in the centre. Stray would ask to see a load of expensive rings. She'd flirt with the owner and distract him. Tracy and Karla would grab the rings. They would throw them into Simone's bag. Simone would throw the bag to me, outside on my bike. I would cycle off, out of the centre. A car would be waiting for me in Crow Lane.

"There's no CCTV in the shop," Simone said. "If we get caught, they'll have nothing on us. It's safe."

"What about Stray? The police have her on file. The jeweller's sure to remember her."

"She won't have done anything wrong," Simone said, with shifty eyes.

"I'm sorry," I said. "I think it's a crap plan. Too risky."

"You're not 16 yet," Stray said. "You can't get into bad trouble."

“No way,” I said. “Can I have a word with you, alone?”

“Anything you say to me you can say in front of my mates,” Stray said.

“You’re going to get caught,” I told her.

“Not if you help.”

“I’m crazy about you,” I whispered, and Simone began to giggle. Karla and Tracy too. “Will I see you tomorrow?”

“Sorry,” Stray said, but her eyes said she was scared. “I have to see Martin, my boyfriend.”

Of course, they did the job without me. I cycled over to the jewellers to see how it went down.

Three girls went inside. No Stray. A moment later, Karla came running out of the shop. She threw a bag to someone on a bike. The cyclist wore a baseball cap and had a scarf round her face. She almost dropped the bag.

A moment later, the alarm went off. I went after the cyclist on my bike. Police sirens filled the shopping centre. The bike wobbled out onto the footpath. The cyclist had a lovely bum but couldn't ride for toffee. I went after her. The alarm kept getting louder, even though we were cycling away from it.

Stray wobbled more and more. She nearly ran into a litter bin. Somehow, she made it to the road. Then a police siren sounded, close by. We both sped up. Stray hit the kerb and fell off the bike. That was when I caught up with her.

"Why do you do the risky stuff?" I asked, helping her up. "Why is it never Simone?"

She gave me a weak smile and held out the bag. "Take it to Martin," she said. "His car's at the end of Crow Lane."

That made me angry. I let go of her arm. I didn't want to hold her. I only wanted to save her.

"Go home," I told Stray. "Quick. Before they catch you."

She took off the cap and her long hair fell down. There was no panic in her dull eyes. What drugs did Martin have her on? Stray handed me the cap and scarf.

"Thanks," she said, and blew me a kiss. Then, slowly, she cycled away.

Chapter 7
Birthday

I did what had to be done. I stayed where I was. A police car zoomed round the corner. I waved at it.

"Another cyclist nearly ran into me," I told the officer. "He dropped this." I handed the bag to the police.

"We'll need a full witness statement," the officer said. "Can you describe the thief?"

"No, but he went that way." I pointed towards Crow Lane, where I hoped Martin was waiting.

"Wait here!" the officer said.

The car zoomed off. As soon as it was out of sight, I cycled off. I didn't see Stray. I hoped she was safe.

Next day, Stray turned up after school, as I was opening my presents. I met her at the door, alone. I didn't invite her in.

"Happy birthday," she said. "I've come for the rings."

"The police were right behind you," I said. "I had to drop the bag."

"You can't have!" Stray cried. "Martin will kill me!"

"Then don't go to him," I said. "Stay with me."

She gave me a sad look. I reached out to her but she took a step back. Then she returned to the waiting car.

Epilogue

All that was seven years ago. When I next saw Stray, she had a black eye. Soon after, she dropped out of sight.

I've been going out with Karen for a year now. We're solid. Last week, we were on holiday in Spain. I bumped into Simone at a bar on the beach. She'd just finished uni.

"I've got a summer job as a travel rep," she said.

"What happened to that old gang of yours?" I asked.

"Don't know," Simone said. "I lost track of them after GCSEs. They were holding me back."

"Do you remember Stray?" I asked.

"You mean Stacey? You don't forget a face like hers. She could have been a model if she'd played her cards right. But Stacey was a mess. She always chose the wrong guys."

"And the wrong friends," I said.

Simone didn't rise to this. "Bet she's got three kids by now," she said. "Or she's in prison. Stray was always being put away."

"Maybe things worked out for her," I said. "Maybe her luck turned."

"You always were a softy," Simone said. "Would you like to meet my boyfriend, Julian? He works in the City."

I said we had to be somewhere else.

"That girl was a right cow," Karen said, when we were alone. "How do you know her?"

And I told her the story I've just told you.

"You always were a softy," Simone said. "Would you like to meet my boyfriend Tolani? He works in the City."

I said we had to be somewhere else.

"That girl was a right cow," Karen said when we were alone. "How do you know her?"

And I told her the story I've just told you.

Barrington Stoke would like to thank all its readers for commenting on the manuscript before publication and in particular:

Lizzie Alder
Callie Brooks
Jane Brooks
Ashley Davis
Mrs Patina Douglas
Joe Gamston
Mrs Julie Gamston
Gregory Godden
Anne-Marie Holder
Alex Johns
Mrs. Hazel Lanceley
Jodie Mathieson
Savahana McNaught
Nicola Mustoe
Alisha Richardson
Kirsty Smith
Blake Teague
Jack Tucker
Daniel Webber
Liam Witherden
Dean Williams

Become a Consultant!

Would you like to give us feedback on our titles before they are published? Contact us at the address below – we'd love to hear from you!

Email: info@barringtonstoke.co.uk
Website: www.barringtonstoke.co.uk